THE STARLIGHT SNOWDOGS

ARCTIC ADVENTURE

Also available:

The Starlight Snowdogs – The Land of Snow

THE STARLIGHT SNOWDOGS

ARCTIC ADVENTURE

Skye Waters

HarperCollins *Children's Books*

For Linda Chapman –
friend and muse

HarperCollins *Children's Books* is a division of HarperCollins *Publishers* Ltd,
77–85 Fulham Palace Road, Hammersmith, London W6 8JB.

Visit our website at: www.harpercollins.co.uk

1 3 5 7 9 10 8 6 4 2
ISBN: 978-0-00-735903-5

Text copyright © Julie Sykes 2011
Cover illustrations copyright © Andrew Farley 2011
Chapter artwork by Tim Stevens

The author asserts the moral right to be identified as the author of the work. A CIP

catalogue record for this title is available from the British Library.

Typeset by Palimpsest Book Production Limited,
Falkirk, Stirlingshire
Printed and bound in England by Clays Ltd, St Ives plc

Mixed Sources
Product group from well-managed
forests and other controlled sources
www.fsc.org Cert no. SW-COC-001806
© 1996 Forest Stewardship Council

FSC is a non-profit international organisation established to promote the
responsible management of the world's forests. Products carrying the FSC
label are independently certified to assure consumers that they come
from forests that are managed to meet the social, economic and
ecological needs of present and future generations.

Find out more about HarperCollins and the environment at
www.harpercollins.co.uk/green

Chapter 1

Ella Edwards poured milk on to her cereal and dreamily stirred it with a spoon. If only she didn't have to go to school this morning! Ella wanted to stay at home and play with Blue, her new husky puppy she'd rescued from a box in the nearby country park. Ella had found Blue a whole week ago, but the excitement of owning a puppy hadn't worn off. She couldn't spend enough time with him!

"Hurry up, Ella," said Mum, putting the milk back in the fridge.

"Sorry," Ella answered, hastily spooning up cornflakes.

She glanced at Blue, dozing in his new dog bed. Suddenly he stiffened, his blue eyes flew open and he pricked up his ears. Then he jumped up and raced for the door, frantically scratching for it to be opened. Ella's spoon clattered into the bowl as she pushed her chair back. Her heart raced with excitement. What was wrong with Blue? Were the Starlight Snow Dogs howling to him? Quickly Ella opened the door and followed Blue into the hall.

Ella had an incredible secret. She was the leader of the Starlight Snowdogs, a magical team of huskies that included Blue. Together, she and her dogs looked after the Arctic, protecting its wildlife from man-made problems. The other five dogs lived in the Arctic and when there was a situation that needed taking care of, they let Blue know by howling. Then Ella was magically whisked away to join the Starlight Snowdogs on a flying sledge pulled by Blue. But as Ella chased Blue along the hall she realised her mistake. Their adventures always started outdoors. Blue hadn't heard the Starlight Snowdogs howling, he was investigating another noise…

Blue had heard the postman.

The letterbox flap opened and the postman jammed three letters through it. Claws skittering on the wood, Blue growled then sprang in the air, deftly catching the letters before they touched the floor.

"Blue, no!" Ella cried.

Blue growled playfully and shook the letters from side to side.

"Leave!" panted Ella, catching him up.

At first Blue refused to drop the letters. Thinking it was a game, he pulled away from Ella.

"Blue, drop!" said Ella, forcing herself to stay calm. Blue didn't mean to be naughty and often his antics were very funny, but he was still on trial; Ella's parents had only agreed to keep him if he behaved himself. Torn post wouldn't help his cause to stay.

"Blue," said Ella sternly. "Drop."

Reluctantly Blue relaxed his grip on the letters, allowing Ella to prise them from his sharp teeth and examine the damage.

"Oh, Blue!" she said, sadly shaking her head.

All three letters had small holes in. Ella sorted through them. Two were junk mail so that didn't matter, but the third was in a brown envelope with a clear window for the address.

A bill, thought Ella.

Luckily the bill had been sandwiched between the other letters so the teeth-shaped

holes weren't as deep as they could have been. Ella smoothed out the creased envelope, then putting it under the junk mail, she went back to the kitchen.

"Post," she said hesitantly.

Mum was rushing round tidying the breakfast things up before she started work.

"Put it on the table. I'll look at it in a minute," she said absently.

Ella breathed a sigh of relief. The envelopes didn't look too bad and with any luck Mum wouldn't notice when she opened them.

Daisy, Ella's big sister, was in a hurry too, ramming things into her school bag.

"Can I take an extra snack? I've got a maths revision class after school, followed by two hours on the ice. We're practising for the figure-skating competition. Katie's mum said she'll drive us to the rink if you can bring us home."

"That's fine," said Mum. "Take some fruit and a bag of crisps."

"Thanks, Mum. Out the way, Blue," said Daisy, stepping over him to get to the cupboard.

Ella finished her cereal and, checking the clock, saw that there were still ten minutes before her own friend Isabel called for her. Enough time to throw a few balls for Blue, who was easily bored and needed lots of entertainment to keep him out of mischief.

"I'll take Blue out in the garden for a bit," she said.

"Good idea," said Mum. "Please can you let the hens out for me? I haven't had time to do it yet."

"OK," said Ella.

Blue gambolled after Ella as she crossed the dew-soaked grass to let Mum's silky bantams, small fluffy hens, out of their hutch. Goldie, the bossiest, stared haughtily at Blue as she marched down the ramp and on to the grass.

"Blue, leave," said Ella firmly, as Blue went to follow her.

Blue only wanted to make friends, but the silky bantams didn't understand and Ella couldn't blame them. Blue left Goldie alone, but put a paw on the ramp to say hello to Cluck, Whisper and Echo.

"Blue," said Ella warningly. She picked up his ball from the grass and threw it for him, adding, "Fetch."

Hens forgotten, Blue eagerly chased after the ball, his long tail curving gracefully over his back. He'd almost reached it when he suddenly accelerated, running past the ball and on towards Dad's vegetable patch.

"You missed it, you mad mutt," said Ella, giggling. "Here, Blue. Fetch the ball."

Blue ignored her and ran on.

"Blue, fetch," said Ella, in a sterner voice.

It was important to follow a command through or Blue wouldn't know when Ella was serious and when she was just playing. Ella stood straight waiting for Blue to return and when he didn't she ran crossly after him.

"Blue, come," Ella reached out and grabbed Blue's collar. Her fingers tingled as they brushed against the silver snowflake dog tag and sank into Blue's thick coat. Then Ella heard something that made the rest of her body fizzle like her fingers – the faint howl of dogs. So Blue hadn't been ignoring her at all. The Starlight Snowdogs were calling them! Ella gripped Blue tighter as he accelerated down the garden. Blue howled and with an indignant squawk Goldie hopped out of his way and hid under a bush.

Ella ran alongside Blue, keeping a tight hold on his collar. As the end of the garden rushed closer, Ella swallowed back the panicky feeling that she and Blue might crash into the fence. At the last minute, Blue's muscles bunched and he launched skyward. Forcing herself to trust that the magic would work, Ella jumped with him, gasping out loud as her breath was sucked from her. Unable to stop herself, Ella looked down. Her stomach somersaulted at the sight of the houses and roads rapidly shrinking away. It made her feel giddy and Ella closed her eyes as she was pulled higher by Blue. When at last she dared to look again, it was pitch black and freezing cold. The wind whipped her face, making her eyes water. There was snow in the air. Ella could smell it even before it came swirling towards her. Soon she was engulfed in a

whirling blanket of icy-white snowflakes that coated her eyelashes and made her blink. Ella hung on to Blue until her fingers were too numb to grip. The wind rushed at her, tearing Blue from her hands. Ella groaned. She knew that Blue would be safe, but she hated this bit when they were temporarily parted. Upside down and alone, Ella spun through the air.

Chapter 2

The wind dropped suddenly, depositing Ella on to a wooden sled. Gratefully she sank back, leaning against the driving bow. The worst was over. This was the fun part of her journey to the Arctic. Ella loved flying through the starlit sky on her magical dog sled pulled by Blue. Sensing her enjoyment, Blue gave a joyful bark. His ears were pricked forward and he carried his black tail with its cute white tip arched proudly over his back.

Magical starlight illuminated the sky and Ella threw out her arms and turned up her face, bathing in its twinkling glow. It was a wonderful feeling and it made her insides fizz. Ella couldn't get enough of it and was disappointed when Blue suddenly dived, pulling the sled downwards until it was engulfed in a swirling array of green and purple lights. The lights twisted across the sky, like long silky maypole ribbons crossing over and under each other so fast that it was impossible to tell where one ended and the other began. Ella's skin glowed green and her hair had a purple sheen, and so did Blue's black and white coat. Whistling and crackling, the lights danced over Ella and Blue. Usually they gave a silent display and Ella eagerly listened to their song as they bathed her and Blue in their magical sparkling glow. Too soon it was over. The ground rushed closer and Ella closed her eyes, her brown hair streaming behind her as the wind tore through it. She braced herself, tightly holding the sides of the sled. There was a gentle bump as Blue landed, then the whoosh of snow as he ran the sled along the ground, decreasing his speed until he was finally able to stop. It took Ella several seconds to get her breath back. Blue stood patiently waiting for her to stop panting, his triangular ears pointing forward and his tail arched. Ella

stared fondly at him. In the Arctic, Blue was still only a puppy, but a larger and older dog than he was at home.

As Ella climbed from the sled she was grateful that during her journey her boring green school uniform had been replaced with a bright red padded coat with a fur-lined hood, matching snow trousers, a thick pair of gloves and sturdy boats. She snuggled deeper into the coat, grateful for its warmth. She didn't recognise where she was, but away to her left she heard a noise. Ella spun round and saw in the distance five husky dogs running towards her at speed. She stood by Blue, excitement welling inside her as the dogs drew closer. Acer reached her first and, stopping a paw's length away, he bowed his head. He was a handsome dog with a glossy black coat, white legs and a white tummy, with a band of black fur across his chest, like a sash. His forehead was black and his face white, the black fur arching like eyebrows and joining in a point between his brown eyes. He was closely followed by his sister Honey, a pretty dog with orangey brown markings and soft brown eyes. Ambitious Bandit was next, but he refused to meet Ella's eyes, staring past her. Ella caught her breath, but didn't have time to dwell on Bandit's continued unfriendliness, as Coda and Inca, arriving last, were clearly pleased to see her. Lovely faithful Coda had waited for Inca, and Ella felt a rush

of affection for him. Blue twitched with pleasure, barely able to conceal his excitement at seeing his sister Inca again.

"Hello, Ella," said Acer, pushing his nose into her hand. "I hope you had a good journey through the Northern Lights?"

"Yes, thank you," said Ella. Acer had never mentioned the Northern Lights before, but before she could ask what they were Acer said, "Good, and now we need your help to move a large wooden crate that we found outside Port Nanuk."

Ella was surprised. In the short time she'd spent in the Arctic, she'd not seen any litter at all. People were careful how they disposed of their rubbish because they didn't want to attract polar bears, as they were dangerous animals, especially when they were hungry.

"Let's go then," she said eagerly.

Immediately the dogs took up their positions in the harness. Ella walked down the line checking that everything was fine. It made her feel good to see the dogs standing with their ears pricked forward with anticipation. All except for Blue, who Ella caught giving Inca a friendly lick on her muzzle. Ella pretended not to notice as she moved on to Coda and Bandit, who always went at the back. Satisfied everything was in order, Ella climbed on to the sled runners and picked up the gangline where it was resting over the curved handrail.

"Hike," she said smartly.

Immediately the dogs took off, running with their ears pricked forward and their tails arched over their backs. It began to snow and soon the craggy mountains, away to Ella's left, vanished in a whirl of whiteness. Something ran across the front of the sledge. Ella leant forward straining to see and just made out an arctic hare, its browny grey coat heavily flecked with white winter fur. Automatically Ella stiffened, worried that Blue might try and chase it. But she'd underestimated him. Here in the Arctic, Blue was a working dog and once the sled was moving he wasn't easily distracted.

The sled sped on, dipping up and down as

it rode the bumps in the landscape. Ella hung on to the driving bow until a long while later she saw buildings in the distance. It looked like Port Nanuk, although Ella wasn't sure as she'd not approached it from this direction before. There were no roads leading to the town, just miles of open snow stretching away like a blank painter's canvas. Then Ella noticed a large object ahead looking very out of place in the bare white landscape.

"Whoa," she called, pulling on the gangline.

Obediently the dogs slowed, stopping a short step from the object, a large wooden crate. Looping the gangline over the driving bow, Ella hopped from the sled and went to investigate.

The crate was sealed with nails and had no markings on it. It was very heavy and barely moved when Ella pushed it. Ella had discovered that here in the Arctic she had magical powers, and one of those powers was strength. She put both hands on the side of the box and cleared her mind. Believing you could do something played a large part in making the magic work. Ella concentrated on the box, convincing herself that she could push it, when suddenly she had a better idea.

"Acer, can you bring the sled closer? It'll be easier if I can lift the crate straight on to it."

Acer barked a command and the dogs stepped forward. Ella put her arms round the crate. It was too wide for her to get a proper grip, but telling herself she could lift it, she took a deep breath and with a straight back bent her knees.

"Think strong," said Acer encouragingly.

Ella concentrated on lifting the box. She knew she had the strength to do it. Then, as her arms began to tingle with magical energy, she lifted it off the snowy ground. It was a struggle at first, but Ella trusted the magic to help her. Her arm muscles tightened like knotty old rope and they prickled like mad, but it wasn't an unpleasant sensation. Grunting loudly Ella carefully transferred the box to the sled.

"Go on," barked Acer.

Ella lowered the box on to the seat.

She was red in the face with exertion and her breath huffed out in a noisy sigh. But she'd done it!

"Well done," said Acer approvingly.

Ella flushed with pleasure, then standing back she studied the box. Now what? She couldn't return it to its owners as there was no way of identifying where it had come from. Maybe she should take it to her new friend Saskia, who lived in Port Nanuk? Saskia would know what to do with the crate. But asking Saskia straight away, without trying to deal with the problem herself, felt like cheating. Ella wanted to have a go on her own. Glancing at the ground she suddenly realised there were tracks in the snow. They weren't very clear as the falling snow was filling them in, but if she hurried she could follow them. Ella noticed that the tracks were much wider than the ones made by her own sled and interestingly they led away from the town.

"If we follow the tracks they might lead us to the owner of this crate," she said to Acer.

Acer seemed pleased with the suggestion. With a surge of excitement Ella climbed back on the runners and picked up the gangline.

"Hike," she said, leaning forward as she urged the dogs on.

As Ella journeyed away from Port Nanuk it stopped snowing. Ella loved the snow, but was pleased it had stopped, as it meant she still had a trail to follow. Keeping her eyes to the

ground she concentrated on following the wide tracks. Sometimes they disappeared completely, then Ella would stop and glance around until she picked the trail up again. Ella hoped she was following the right trail, but didn't think there would be too many people travelling out here. Soon she heard a whispering noise that grew steadily louder. Ella kept going until the whispering revealed itself as a wide river. The water was semi-frozen and chunks of ice clanked against the banks. Ella and her dog team followed alongside the river for ages until the tracks snaked one way and the river flowed in the opposite direction. The dogs pulled Ella up a hill, then effortlessly slid down the other side.

The landscape here was bleak with a few distinctive-looking trees dotted about. There were three that looked like people gossiping and one with a dramatic Y-shaped trunk. Ella urged the dogs on until far in the distance she saw a thick forest of coniferous trees.

"Look!" she cried, excitedly pointing at a curl of smoke rising from them.

"A camp fire in the forest."

Chapter 3

Excitement gave Ella a new energy and she pushed the dogs on. They ran faster, their harness creaking and their paws crunching in the fresh snow. The forest was further away than it looked and for a while Ella thought they would never reach it, but eventually they drew close enough to see inside. Suddenly Ella wished there was another route to follow.

The forest looked dark and uninviting. What if polar bears were sheltering in there? The dogs hesitated, sensing Ella's nervousness.

Bravely she urged them on, calling, "Hike."

They entered the trees and Ella slowed the dogs to a walk. It was an eerie place to make a camp. The forest seemed too quiet. There was none of the rustling of unseen creatures like there was in the Country Park near Ella's home. Hoping that she would be able to find her way back, Ella steered the dogs deeper. A little while later she heard an unfamiliar noise. Ella suppressed a shiver. Whatever was going on?

"Whoa," she whispered.

The dogs stopped immediately, ears pricked waiting for their next command.

Acer threw back his head, his whiskers twitching as he sniffed the air.

"I can hear a machine. And I can smell smoke," said Ella quietly. "We must be nearly at the camp."

She climbed off the sled saying, "Wait here while I take a closer look."

"Be careful," Acer warned her.

Swallowing back her nerves Ella crept through the trees. Soon she heard voices – a man and a lady, both with strong Canadian accents, were talking earnestly. Using the trees for cover Ella crept closer until she reached the edge of a clearing and stopped in surprise. She'd stumbled upon a camp consisting of several sturdy tents, three snowmobiles and a large amount of machinery. Her eyes widened as she took it all in. There were cylinders, pipes, a small generator and a large red machine that looked like a portable drill. It was the drill that was making the noise. Ella stared at it for ages, but she couldn't work out what it was drilling for. In one corner of the camp were several wooden boxes, all identical to the one Ella had found. One box was open and inside was a mountain of cooking utensils and tins of food. The man and the lady were still talking, sitting round a camp fire clutching mugs. Ella listened to them for a bit, but the conversation didn't make any sense as it was full of unfamiliar words that she guessed must be

connected to the machinery. But at least she'd found out who owned the crate. Ella guessed it contained supplies and it had obviously fallen from the vehicle that had transported all the other things here. Eager to share her news with the Starlight Snowdogs she made her way back to her sled.

"What will you do now?" asked Acer, when Ella finished telling him what she'd discovered.

Ella thought about it. She didn't want the drilling team to know she was there in case they asked awkward questions. No one had actually said that the Starlight Snowdogs were a secret, but instinctively Ella knew they were.

"I know," she said at last. "I'll leave the crate on the edge of the camp for the people to find."

"Won't they wonder how it got there?" piped up Blue.

"They'll probably think that's where they lost it," said Ella.

"What are they doing?" asked Honey curiously.

"They're drilling for something." Ella wished she knew what. The hidden camp had made her feel uneasy. "Acer, how far can you take the sled without being heard?"

"Right up to the clearing," said Acer confidently.

"Let's go," said Ella, leading the way.

On silent paws the dogs stepped forward, pulling the sled behind them. At the edge of the clearing Ella put up her hand for them to stop. Once more she leant over the crate and cleared her mind of everything else.

I can do this, she told herself.

Blue was watching Ella and tilted his head in encouragement. Ella smiled back. Her confidence was so strong that she lifted the box as easily as if it was a box of tissues. She put it on the ground, then stood back. She was hot with exertion and unzipped her coat a short way, welcoming the feel of the chilly air on her neck. The dogs watched her expectantly, waiting for their next command. Silently Ella pointed back the way they'd come. There wasn't much room to turn, but with a few shunts they managed it and, once the sled was facing in the right direction, Ella climbed on to its runners with her hands resting on the driving bow. No one spoke until they were out of the forest and back in the open.

The weak autumn sunlight reflected off the snow, dazzling Ella. She screwed up her eyes and called, "Easy," to the dogs, who immediately slowed down.

Ella was pleased she'd found the crate's owners, but a niggling feeling told her that her task wasn't over. Her initial surprise and unease at finding a drilling camp in the middle of nowhere had now turned to suspicion.

Exactly what were the people looking for and how would their activities affect the Arctic wildlife? There was one person Ella knew who might have the answers to her questions.

"Acer," she called. "Can we go to Port Nanuk? I want to talk to Saskia."

"Yes, of course," said Acer.

Ella guided the sled back the way they'd come and although the tracks she'd followed earlier had been wiped out with fresh snow she recognised certain landmarks. There was the coniferous, Y-shaped tree, the three trees huddled together like gossiping friends and the gently sloping hill. The dogs were panting as they reached the top and Ella called them to a halt to let them catch their breath. There was an amazing view from up here. A bubbling feeling rose in Ella's stomach as she stared at the brilliant white world stretching before her. It was so beautiful and so unspoilt. Leading the Starlight Snowdogs and experiencing this wild landscape was the most wonderful thing ever. For a split second Ella wished that Isabel was there to share it with her too. But at least she had Saskia. Ella couldn't wait to see her new friend again. Gathering up the gangline she prepared to send the dogs forward, but before she could, something caught her eye. A long dark line that from this distance resembled marching ants was heading towards the river from the opposite direction. Ella stared in fascination

until the ant-like figures grew large enough to make out.

"Caribou!" she exclaimed in wonder.

There were so many it was almost impossible to tell where one ended and the next began.

"Where are they going?" Ella asked.

"They're moving to their winter ground," Acer explained. "In the summer they live in the north where the mosquitoes are fewer and there's a plentiful supply of lichen for their newborn calves. In the winter they return to the south, where the climate is milder and there is a fresh supply of food."

The herd moved steadily towards the river in an orderly line. The adults were easy to spot with their enormous velvety antlers. The calves were much smaller and their growing antlers resembled twigs. Ella had never seen such an enormous herd of animals and was so impressed she stood staring at the caribou as they calmly picked their way towards the river. It was a complete surprise when, without faltering, the lead animals waded into the water and, thrusting their heads forward, began to swim. The river was fast flowing, carrying chunks of ice that clunked against each other. The caribou didn't swim straight across it. Instead they snaked their way to the opposite bank, making wide serpentine loops. Ella held her breath, fearful that they wouldn't make the journey safely.

"Why are they swimming like that?" she asked. "Won't it take longer to cross?"

Bandit sniggered and Acer gave him a low warning growl before answering.

"The current makes it impossible to swim in a straight line."

"Of course," said Ella, feeling slightly silly.

All she could see of the swimming caribou were their thrusting heads and occasionally their stumpy tails bobbing in the water as they struck out for the opposite bank. There seemed no end to the herd. As more animals launched themselves into the water there were others filling their place on the land. Ella's eyes flickered from the caribou swimming in the semi-frozen river to the long line of animals still crossing the snow-covered land to reach it. There were hundreds of caribou ranging from the very young to the very old. It seemed a long while before the first swimmers approached the shore. Nimbly they scrambled out of the river, picking their way across the rocks and continuing their journey on land like an unstoppable army.

"Lucky they're going the opposite way to us," said Ella half to herself. It was going to take ages for the whole herd to be clear of the river and she was getting cold. She wriggled her fingers inside her padded gloves and then wiggled her toes, but even though she was wearing cosy thick socks her feet still felt numb.

"Hike," she said reluctantly, knowing if she stayed where she was she would freeze.

Eagerly the dogs moved forward. Acer and Honey needed little guidance as they surefootedly made their way down the hill, Ella struggling to tear her eyes away from the spectacular sight of the migrating caribou. Soft grunts rang out in the distance, until a sudden bellow made Ella twist her head in surprise.

"No!" she gasped.

A young caribou was being swept away by the river. Eyes rolling with fright, it frantically kicked at the icy water. With heart-wrenching bellows its mother swam after it. The rest of the herd ignored the drama and continued on their way, elegantly rising from the water as they reached the shore and tiptoeing across the rocks. Ella gathered up the gangline. There was no way she could watch the calf drown. She had to rescue it.

Chapter 4

"**H**ike!" Ella shouted, leaning across the driving bow. "Hike!"

The dogs tensed, but didn't move.

"Hike!" cried Ella wildly. "Hurry, Acer, the calf needs our help."

Acer stood proud, his triangular ears pricked forward, his plumed tail arched over his back. Ella was confused. She knew Acer could hear her, so why was he refusing to move on? She jumped from the sled runners and ran along the line of dogs until she was in front of him.

"What's wrong?" she asked frantically. "Why won't you help me? Is this something I have to do by myself?"

Ella was aware of Blue and Honey's sympathetic looks and Bandit's scornful stance. But she didn't care how stupid she sounded. All that mattered was saving the caribou calf.

"Tell me what to do," she begged.

Carefully Acer scraped a hole in the snow with his front paw.

"I'm sorry, Ella," he said at last. "This isn't

a matter for the Starlight Snowdogs. The problem is a natural one, not something that's been caused by humans. Harsh as it seems, we must let nature take its course."

Ella was shocked. Why did they have to let nature take its course? For a few crazy seconds she thought about ignoring Acer and going to help the calf anyway. But as she went to move a thought occurred to her. Would her magical powers work if she wasn't acting with the Starlight Snowdogs? Ella had more than a suspicion they wouldn't and deep down she knew she mustn't interfere with nature. This was a battle the calf must fight on its own.

Ella didn't want to watch the calf drown,

but at the same time she had to know its fate. Bravely she turned to the river where the calf was battling against the current. It was a fighter! As the river swept it downstream, the calf frenziedly kicked its legs. Its mother swam after it, but was unable to catch up. Ella clenched her hands making fat gloved fists as she silently urged the calf on. She was dimly aware of Blue leaning against her leg in a comforting way, with Honey sitting on the other side. Grateful for their support, Ella rested one hand on Blue's black and white head and the other on Honey's orangey brown back. Several tense minutes passed before miraculously the calf began to hold its own against the ice-filled river. With small

determined strokes it began to gain ground. Slowly but surely the calf paddled closer to the shore. It was a treacherous journey. Several times the calf was swept back, but it refused to give up and finally it was able to stand in the rushing water. On trembling legs it scrambled over the rocks until it was finally clear of the river. Its mother followed close behind, gently nudging the calf to safety.

"It's done it!" cheered Ella ecstatically.

She expected the calf and its mother to stop and rest for a while, but they kept on going, joining the herd as it continued its long trek south for the winter. Now Ella was the one with shaky legs as she climbed back on to the sled runners. Inca wagged her tail as Ella passed and Blue gave her a swift lick on the hand.

"Working dog or pet?" hissed Bandit unkindly, but Blue ignored him.

Ella stared at Bandit. She couldn't work him out. It was obvious he didn't like her. He'd made that clear from the start. But why? What had she done? Ella had no idea and longed to ask him, but she wanted to talk in private and so far there hadn't been that opportunity.

"Hike," she called, bracing herself as the sled slid forward.

Wrapped in her thoughts about Bandit, Ella barely noticed the ride to Port Nanuk.

The dogs slowed as they entered the town, their claws pattering as they went from the soft snow to the hard, ice-packed road. There were a few people about, but no one paid Ella any attention as she drove along. She wasn't familiar enough with Port Nanuk to find her way to Saskia's house, so she held the gangline lightly, letting Acer steer. Soon Acer and Honey turned right into a long street and Ella recognised Saskia's house halfway down it. Would Saskia be in? Ella hoped so and eagerly craned forward. There was a sudden whooshing sound then something smacked her in the shoulder exploding in a cloud of white. A snowball! Ella grinned delightedly. She loved a good snowball fight.

"Whoa," she called, slowing the dogs as she glanced round to see who the opposition was.

But apart from a lady dressed in a long coat with a baby tucked in her hood there was no one else around. There were plenty of places for a snowball thrower to hide though, with several of the houses having parked cars outside them.

Wumph!

Another snowball hit Ella on her shoulder with considerably more force than the first. It was quickly followed by two more both hitting her squarely on her chest.

"Truce," called Ella, pulling the dogs to a halt and searching the area the snowballs had

come from. "Let me make some snowballs and then we can have a proper fight."

Maybe the snowball thrower didn't understand truce, for suddenly Ella was bombarded with snowballs. It would have been funny if the attack had been friendly, but clearly it wasn't. Snowballs rained down on Ella, hitting her with such force that even her padded clothes weren't enough to stop them stinging.

Without being told, the dogs moved on, hurrying down the street to Saskia's house. Ella clutched the driving bow in shock. It felt like the snowball thrower was trying to stop her from reaching Saskia's. But that was stupid. Why would anyone do that? She didn't know anyone here apart from Saskia.

"Gee," called Ella as they drew up alongside Saskia's long, salmon-coloured house with the pointed roof.

The Starlight Snowdogs didn't need to be told to turn right. Eagerly they pulled off the road and ran down the side of the house. Ella was hit one last time on the back by a snowball before reaching the safety of the yard. The dogs stood to attention, softly panting as steam rose from their heaving sides. Ella brushed the snow from her coat, then jumping off the sled said, "Free."

The harness magically fell off the dogs and as they rolled together in the snow Blue ran to Ella and pushed his nose in her hand.

"Are you all right?" he asked, his voice full of concern.

"Yes," said Ella, "What—"

But before she could ask her question, the back door of the house opened and Saskia ran down the steps towards her.

"You're back!" she cried, swiftly hugging her.

A warm glow spread through Ella as she hugged Saskia. At least someone was pleased to see her!

Saskia held Ella at arm's length to study her. Shyly Ella glanced at her Inuit friend with her interesting weather-beaten face and her black hair caught back in a neat ponytail.

"It's good to see you," said Saskia. "Come inside and tell me what you've been up to while I make you a hot drink."

"Thanks," said Ella, conscious that her voice sounded very English against Saskia's strong Canadian accent.

She glanced at the dogs. Acer and Honey had finished rolling in the snow and were happily slumped together, nibbling at their paws. Coda lay with them, a wistful expression in his dark brown eyes as he watched Blue and Inca play fighting. Bandit was nowhere to be seen. Ella wondered if she should go and find him, but then she remembered that Bandit had disappeared the last time she'd visited Saskia.

"I wonder where he goes," thought Ella vaguely as she followed Saskia indoors.

Chapter 5

Saskia had been baking and the kitchen smelt lovely. Ella peeled off her outer clothes and hung them on the back of a chair, then sat down. Music was playing in the background — a rhythmic chanting, two voices panting out unfamiliar sounds in alternating deep and high-pitched voices. Ella had never heard anything like it and the music called to her, filling her head and making her skin prickle. Unconsciously she rocked in her seat, moving in time with the chanting. She was so lost in the strange sounds that when Saskia put a mug of hot chocolate down in front of her she jumped.

"You like the music?" asked Saskia, smiling.

"Erm, yes," stuttered Ella, feeling slightly dazed. "What is it?"

"Inuit throat singing."

Saskia placed a tray of warm chocolate brownies on the table and indicated for Ella to take one. "Throat singing is an ancient tradition. Long ago Inuit women sang for fun when the men were out hunting, often competing to see if they could outdo each other. It was also a way of passing on news."

"Can you throat sing?" asked Ella curiously.

"Yes, my mother taught me. It's quite difficult. You breathe in on the high notes and out on the deep ones. Jak's good at it. He caught on very quickly when I taught him."

"Jak?" questioned Ella. She thought she'd heard the name before, but she couldn't remember where.

"Jaiku is my grandson. We call him Jak for short. He lives here with his parents. They're in the tourist industry and they work long shifts, so Jak and I spend lots of time together. School's closed today and he's gone out with his friends, but I expect you'll meet him soon. I hope so."

Ella hoped so too. It would be fun to make a friend her own age. She bit into a chocolate brownie. It was warm and crumbly on the outside with a delicious gooey centre. The music came to an end and Saskia reached out and switched the hi-fi system off.

"Does Jak know about the Starlight Snowdogs?" asked Ella suddenly.

"Yes… he does."

Saskia stared into her mug, giving Ella the strong impression that she was hiding something, but before she could pursue it Saskia asked her, "What have you done today?"

"I saw caribou," said Ella. "There were hundreds of them. It was amazing."

Eagerly she launched into a description of

her day, starting from the beginning and the recovery of the mysterious crate; then finding the drilling company in the woods; and finally the drama of the caribou calf that almost got swept down the icy river.

"It must have been hard knowing you were unable to help the caribou," said Saskia.

"It was," said Ella, recalling her frustration. Saskia chuckled.

"Everything comes with rules, even magic."

"I need a list," Ella joked. Then she could stop embarrassing herself in front of Bandit.

"Inuit laws are remembered, but never written down. If the paper is torn then the rules are gone," said Saskia wisely. "It's the same for magic."

Ella thought about this in silence and decided she liked the idea. Some things in life were instinctive and didn't need to be written on paper. Magic was definitely one of those things.

"Do you know anything about the drilling in the woods?" she asked at last.

Saskia sighed.

"It's an exploratory mining team that's looking for diamonds."

"Diamonds!" Ella was impressed. "Well I hope they don't find them," she added quickly. "They're already ruining the place with their machinery."

"In many ways you're right," Saskia agreed. "But it isn't all bad. If diamonds are found then it will create a great many opportunities for the people that live here. There's hardly anyone who follows the old way of life, living on the land as hunter-gatherers. Yes, we still fish and we hunt seals and caribou, but it's hard to survive like that and we all want an easier life. The diamond company will create opportunities that will be good for us if we work together to ensure a sympathetic approach. There're lots of ways to protect the wildlife while the mining takes place."

"Maybe I could help," said Ella. It sounded just the thing she should be doing as the leader of the Starlight Snowdogs.

"I'm sure you will," Saskia stood up and carried her mug to the sink. "Would you like another drink?"

"No, thanks." Ella felt happily full. "I suppose I'd better go home."

She cleared the table then put on her outdoor clothes.

"See you soon," said Saskia, opening the back door.

As Ella stepped outside Bandit gambolled into the back yard followed by a boy about her own age wearing a navy blue parka with a thick fur-lined hood. The boy had a round smiley face, deep brown eyes and black hair. He was throwing snowballs for Bandit, who leapt about snapping at them like a puppy.

"Jak!" exclaimed Saskia happily. "You're back. Come and meet Ella."

Jak swung round and when he saw Ella coming down the steps from the back door he scowled. Ella's insides dipped and she flushed with discomfort. What had she done to provoke a reaction like that?

"Hello." Jak's eyes slid past Ella, then running his hand down Bandit's back, he ran indoors.

"Ella, I'm sorry," Saskia apologised. "I'm sure he didn't mean to be rude."

"It's fine," said Ella, not wanting to make a big thing of it. She called to the dogs, saying goodbye to each of them in turn so that Saskia wouldn't see how embarrassed she felt. Had it been Jak who'd ambushed her with snowballs earlier? Ella had a strong feeling that he didn't want her around, but surely he wouldn't have attacked her? Bandit stood stiffly and Ella had a sudden thought.

"You're Jak's dog, aren't you?" she asked him.

"Yes," said Bandit, his eyes softening. He was a handsome dog with striking markings; his black head contrasting sharply with his white face with the black line that extended all the way from his brow to the tip of his nose. And those very bandit-like black rings round his eyes.

Ella nodded, suddenly understanding Bandit's attitude to her, but still bewildered as to why Jak didn't like her. Coda, standing next to Bandit, gave Ella a friendly tail wag when it was his turn to say goodbye. Gratefully Ella patted the top of his dark grey head before moving on to Inca, who thrust her nose out and licked Ella's gloved hands.

Ella giggled as she patted Inca. Reluctantly she sent Blue to his harness and checked the tugline – the rope that attached the harness to the main part of the gangline. Satisfied that everything was right, Ella climbed on to the sled in the passenger's seat. She couldn't put it off any longer. It was time to go home.

Waving to Saskia she called to Blue, "It's time to go. Hike, Blue."

At once Blue moved forward, carefully

pulling the sled round the side of the house. His paws clicked on the icy road as he ran faster, gathering speed to overtake a parked car.

"Have you enjoyed yourself?" he called back to Ella.

"I've had a brilliant time," she agreed. "What about you?"

"Me too," said Blue happily.

"Do you miss living here?" Ella immediately regretted her impulsive question. Did she really want to hear Blue's answer?

"Living with you more than makes up for the things I miss," said Blue.

Ella swallowed back the lump that was suddenly in her throat, but before she could

tell Blue how much his words meant, cold air rushed at her and they were airborne. Ella's stomach dipped as she leant over the side watching the snow-clad houses growing smaller. A sudden flash of green light lit up the sky, then everything turned black. The wind caught Ella's light brown hair and blew it over her face. She pushed it back, but the wind caught it again so Ella gave up, and with Blue's words echoing in her ears she settled back to enjoy the ride home.

Time had no meaning as Ella soared through the air in a magical black void. But too soon the sled began to drop. Hanging on tightly Ella braced herself to land. The ground rushed nearer, then suddenly she was falling through the air. Ella landed in the garden next to her den. Blue dropped down beside her with a triumphant howl. For a second Ella's mind was still in the Arctic. She stroked Blue's head as she reluctantly forced her thoughts back to her home. What had she been doing before she was whisked away to join the Starlight Snowdogs?

"School!" groaned Ella.

Checking her watch she saw that it was almost time to leave.

"Come on, Blue. The party's over!" said Ella, heading indoors.

Chapter 6

School seemed very boring after Ella's exciting trip to the Arctic. In maths Ella's thoughts kept slipping to caribou and in literacy she kept remembering the drilling team camping out in the snowy woodland site. She wondered about Jak too. What had she done to make him dislike her so much? Or had she overreacted? Maybe Jak was shy and that's why he'd behaved in an unfriendly manner?

At the end of the day Ella stuffed her belongings back into her bag and was the first out of the classroom.

"Wait for me," called Isabel.

Ella waited impatiently while her friend packed her things away and wriggled into the straps of her backpack.

"Mum and I are taking my little brothers to the park," said Isabel. "Do you want to come too? Billy's got a new football."

"No, thanks," said Ella. "I'm going to start training Blue on his new lead."

"But you're not allowed to take him for walks. He hasn't had all his injections," said Isabel.

"I'm training him in the garden. It takes a while for some puppies to get used to walking on the lead so I thought I'd start now," Ella replied.

Isabel looked wistful.

"That sounds fun."

"Come home with me then," Ella said. "You can ring your mum from my house and tell her where you are."

Isabel hesitated.

"I'd better not. You know what my brothers are like and Mum gives me extra pocket money for helping her with them."

"Another time then," said Ella.

They walked past the Country Park and Ella felt a thrill of excitement that soon she'd

be able to take Blue there for proper walks. Then the girls parted and Ella ran the rest of the way home, keen to get started with Blue's lesson.

But first there was a mess to clear up in the kitchen.

While Mum had been busy working in her home office, Blue had grown bored and started a fight with his new bed.

"Oh, Blue," said Ella sadly, shaking her head. She picked up the quilt that went inside and held it out to Blue, showing him the large hole with the stuffing poking through.

"Naughty," she said sternly. "No, Blue."

Blue wouldn't look at Ella, but lay flat on the ground with his head resting between his

paws. He knew he'd been naughty and looked as if he was trying to disappear through the stone floor tiles.

"I know," said Ella, hating having to tell him off. "You chew because you're bored. But it won't be long before I can take you out for long walks."

The damage wasn't as bad as it looked. Ella pushed the stuffing back inside the quilt and put it in the bed with the hole at the back so no one would notice.

"I'll sew it up later," she told Blue, as she collected his lead from the utility room.

The moment she opened the back door Blue ran outside. Ella hurried after him and caught him up as he stopped to sniff round the hens'

coop. As Ella reached for Blue's collar her hand brushed against his silver snowflake tag. The snowflake was incredibly cold and pulsed like it was full of tiny electrical charges. Ella's fingers tingled and excitement coursed through her. Her latest trip to the Arctic had gone well, but Ella knew she mustn't over-congratulate herself. She still had lots to learn about her new magical skills and how to apply them. Deftly Ella clipped Blue's lead on to his collar, then tugging it gently she said, "Blue, come on."

Blue's head jerked round in surprise. He stared at Ella and when she pulled the lead again he plonked his bottom firmly on the ground.

"Blue, come," said Ella, swallowing a giggle.

This wasn't a game and it was important not to give Blue the wrong impression.

Blue refused to move so Ella pulled gently on the lead. Blue slid towards her, looking surprised and indignant, then he scrambled up and stood firmly with his paws squarely apart.

"Come on," said Ella.

At first Blue wouldn't walk. Ella kept gently tugging the lead and calling to him. After a while Blue took a tiny step and, realising nothing bad was going to happen, he took another.

"Good boy."

Ella gave Blue lots of encouragement as she coaxed him around the garden. He didn't always want to go the same way as her and several times he sat down and refused to move. Ella didn't get cross. Patiently she talked to him until Blue gave in and followed her again. Ella finished the lesson on a good note when Blue had walked the length of the garden with her. She let him off the lead and Blue immediately rolled on his back and waved his paws in the air.

"Good boy," said Ella, rubbing his tummy.

Blue grunted with pleasure, then righting himself, he licked Ella on the nose. Ella hugged him and they tumbled in the grass together until Mum called her in for tea. Daisy was still ice skating, but Dad was home and over the meal Ella told him about Blue's lesson.

"When Blue's on the lead, make sure he walks by your side. The command is 'Heel'," said Dad helpfully.

Ella wanted to practise some more after tea, but Dad thought that Blue had done enough for the day.

"You can clear the table and stack the dishwasher," said Mum, as she rushed out to pick up Daisy and Katie from their ice-skating class.

Ella finished her chores, then spent the rest of the evening sewing up Blue's dog bed. The following morning Ella was pouring cornflakes into a bowl when Blue's ears pricked up.

"Postman," said Daisy, jumping up and racing Blue into the hall. Remembering how Blue had attacked the letters Ella ran after them. She needn't have worried. Daisy reached the post first and held it up triumphantly.

"Beat you!" she said to Blue. She sifted through the letters until she reached the packet at the bottom.

"Mr Andrew Edwards," she read, her face falling. "Rats, I thought it was for me."

"What were you expecting?" asked Ella inquisitively.

"My new competition dress," said Daisy. "Mum ordered it on the Internet. It's beautiful, hot red with hundreds of gold sequins. I can't wait to skate in it."

Daisy took the post to the kitchen and gave it to Mum.

"Thanks, Daisy. It makes a nice change not to have teeth marks in my post."

"No problem," said Daisy, going back to her breakfast.

"Don't think I didn't notice yesterday's damaged letters," Mum continued, glancing pointedly at Blue.

Ella's heart skipped a beat. Was Mum about to give Blue a warning?

But Mum fell silent as she opened a letter and began to read it.

"Thank goodness for that," murmured Ella. She'd have to watch Blue more carefully. He'd got away with it this time, but would Mum be so forgiving if he did it again?

Chapter 7

The school day dragged on. Ella struggled to concentrate on her work and not worry about Blue and what mischief he might be getting up to. They did vaulting in PE and Ella grew frustrated with herself when she was unable to jump over the box. She'd done much bigger jumps in the Arctic! Maths was the worst lesson though. It was so boring and Ella's head ached from puzzling over the sums she was given to solve. She was relieved when the home-time bell went and thrilled when her teacher forgot to give the class any homework. Ella rushed out of the classroom in case Mrs Knight suddenly realised her mistake.

She arrived home to find Blue was waiting for her, wagging his tail and squeaking with excitement as she came in. He nudged her across the kitchen with his nose until they were at the back door. Then he began scratching to go out. The door was locked and as Ella fumbled with the key Blue howled sharply. Ella reached out and as her fingers sank into his soft double coat of fur she heard dogs howling in the distance. Ella's face lit up with a huge smile as she wrenched open the door. It was time! The Starlight Snowdogs were calling her and Blue.

"Let's go," she said, piling out of the back door. Blue surged ahead and Ella snatched at his collar, determined not to be left behind.

Spooks, the elderly cat, was sunning himself on the top of the hen house and hissed in alarm as Ella and Blue tore past. Ella felt like she was running on air as she sped by Dad's vegetable patch, heading towards the fence at the end of the garden. Muscles straining, Blue jumped, pulling Ella up with him. She swooped upwards, hanging on to Blue with both hands, feeling like her stomach had overtaken her mouth as he effortlessly pulled her higher. Home was now a tiny dot in the distance along with all the other houses and gardens in Ella's street. Ella's arms and legs were everywhere and she closed her eyes and forced her protesting muscles to relax. She kept her eyes shut until the air turned freezing cold and when she opened them again she found herself flying through a coal-black sky with an icy wind helping her along. This time there was no snow, but the cold was the worst Ella had ever experienced. She gritted her teeth, gaining some comfort from the warmth of Blue's fur until she lost all feeling in her fingers. Seconds later the wind tore Blue away from her. Alone, Ella somersaulted through the sky until the wind suddenly dropped and she fell like a stone. She landed with a thud on her magical wooden sled and, huffing with relief, thankfully leant back against the driving bow. Now for the fun part of the journey! Ella threw out her arms, lapping up the beautiful starlit sky as Blue effortlessly flew on. The starlight grew stronger, bathing Ella in a magical glow. Ella felt warm and bubbly inside, as if the magic was filling her up ready for her next task in the Arctic. A long while later Blue dived, pulling the sled down at an alarming rate. Ella gripped the sled's sides, then suddenly mysterious green lights danced towards her. Ella loved the lights and the long green

ribbons they made in the sky, twirling and whirling with the grace of a ballerina. Blue's coat and Ella's hair sparkled green and Ella felt a rush of magic surging along the light ribbons and into her tingling body. Then it was over. Blue dived and the ground raced up to meet them. Ella pressed her feet into the sled as if she could help Blue brake. They landed with a bump on hard ice, sliding crazily until Blue regained his footing and brought the sled to a halt. Ella's legs shook as she climbed off and walked to Blue's head.

"Well done," she said.

Blue's ear twitched, then he sat perfectly still. Ella thought how dignified he looked with both ears pricked and his white-tipped tail arched over his back. It was freezing cold, but Blue didn't seem to notice. Sinking deeper into her coat Ella pulled up her fur-lined hood. She heard the Starlight Snowdogs before she saw them, their paws softly crunching in the snow and the rhythmic panting of their collective breaths. Ella resisted the urge to lay a hand on Blue's head. She waited patiently while inside, her stomach fizzed with anticipation. What would she have to do today?

Acer was in the lead with Honey and Bandit a paw length behind. Coda was next, then Inca, her paws working faster than the other dogs, a determined look on her black and white face that was so like Blue's. Bandit

was struggling too, but with the effort of not overtaking Acer. The dogs ran straight at Ella and Blue, but Ella trusted them to stop and they did a whisker in front of her.

"Welcome," said Acer, his voice loud and clear although his mouth never moved.

Blue dipped his head respectfully and Ella said, "Hello."

"We've found an injured caribou," said Acer, coming straight to the point. "We think it's been shot and it's struggling to keep up with the herd."

A thousand thoughts flashed through Ella's mind, but there was no time for questions. With a short bark Acer called the dogs to take up their positions to pull the sled. Ella noticed, as she checked the harnesses, that partners Bandit and Coda had swapped sides.

"You're in the wrong place," she said, stopping alongside them.

Bandit's lips curled into a sneer, but Coda hurriedly said, "We swap places occasionally. It makes us think about what we're doing and if one of us gets injured then someone else can take that position."

"Thanks," said Ella, running her hand down Coda's thick neck.

Coda looked pleased and Bandit pointedly stared in the other direction.

Inca and Blue had also changed sides and they gave Ella a swift lick on her gloved hand as she checked their lines. Satisfied that

everything was in the right place Ella climbed on to the sled runners calling, "Hike."

The dogs moved smoothly forward, gathering speed until they were running flat out. Racing across the snowy landscape was a completely different experience to flying across the sky, but Ella loved it just as much. She hung on to the driving bow, keeping a light touch on the gangline and using her body weight to steer. Away to the right Ella could see the glint of water and soon she realised it was the river and they were on a parallel path to the one she'd travelled on her last visit. After a while the ground began to slope upwards. The snow was powdery and much deeper than it had been before and the dogs slowed as their paws sunk into it. Ella wondered if she should walk up the hill, but the sled was moving too fast for her to jump off and there wasn't time to stop. She leant forward, rising on the balls of her feet as if somehow that would lessen the load. Nearing the top of the hill Ella saw bright red drops of blood staining the snow. Acer and Honey slowed and Ella was able to jump from the sled.

"We must be close," she said, pointing at the marks.

"The herd is on the other side of the hill," Acer quietly replied.

The enormity of the situation suddenly hit Ella. How badly injured was the caribou and

would she have the skill to help it? Ella pushed the thoughts away, refusing to think about failure. The first thing was to find which caribou was injured. Remembering the size of the herd Ella thought that could be difficult and she approached the top of the hill with trepidation. Caribou were alert creatures and Ella knew they would sense her presence by sound and scent, if the wind was in the right direction. Walking quietly in clumpy boots was difficult but not impossible. Ella placed her feet as soundlessly as she could. At the top of the hill she stopped and her eyes widened at the incredible sight before her. Halfway down the slope hundreds of caribou were stretched out across the hillside as the herd steadily

made their way to the bottom. A few stragglers remained on the upper slopes and to Ella's delight she noticed the injured animal limping along at the back. But her delight quickly turned to concern at the bright red trail the caribou left in its wake.

Chapter 8

Ella hesitated, unsure if she should carry on with the dogs or go by herself.

"Caribou are very sensible. If there's an unfamiliar object around they'll either ignore it or go and investigate. They'll only take flight if they feel threatened," said Acer suddenly.

Ella nodded and deciding she felt more comfortable approaching the injured caribou on foot than on the sled she carried on walking.

"Hike," she called softly, asking her dog team to join her as she made her way down the hill.

Ella placed her feet carefully to avoid slipping and frightening the injured caribou, who kept giving her nervous looks over its shoulder. Concerned that she might spook the animal into taking flight Ella gave it plenty of room, approaching it in a wide arc. At last she was level with the caribou, but she carried on walking until she was ahead by several sled lengths.

"Whoa," she called, stopping the dogs and perching on the edge of the sled.

She stared into the distance, watching the caribou from the corner of her eye so it didn't feel intimidated. The dogs sat quietly, Blue and Inca lying on their bellies, taking advantage of the stop to have a rest. The caribou hesitated then slowly approached until it was close enough for Ella to see the flesh wound in its chest. Although she'd never had any dealings with guns before, it was clear that the caribou had been shot. A shallow wound across its chocolate-brown fur suggested the bullet had only grazed the skin and wasn't stuck in the creature. Blood dripped like a leaky tap splashing from the caribou's chest on to its wide hoof and dripping on to the snow.

"Hello," whispered Ella, feeling slightly foolish, but wanting to make contact.

The caribou tensed, and rolling its eyes it threw up its head as if it might run away.

"Steady," Ella whispered. Her heart was banging against her chest and her legs felt wobbly. The caribou was smaller than a horse, but it was as tall as Ella and its impressive antlers made it seem enormous. She hoped it was friendly. Ella didn't reckon her chances if it charged at her now. Gradually the caribou lowered its head until it was staring straight at her.

Still as a stone she waited, staring back at the animal, willing it to understand that she meant no harm.

"I'm here to help," Ella thought silently, though how she was supposed to heal a gunshot wound she had no idea.

The caribou huffed out its breath forming a steam cloud that hovered in the air between them. It glanced at Ella and suddenly they locked eyes. Ella felt strange. A hot flush spread through her body. It was accompanied by a low sound that reminded her of chanting. The sound grew louder, carrying her with it like a surfer riding a wave. In time with the chanting, Ella rocked backwards and forwards hearing the music swelling in her head, a breathy noise of low then high notes, as if the Inuit singer was panting a message to her. As the song continued Ella imagined the caribou healthy and strong and running with the herd. The image was so strong it was as if she was running with the caribou too, galloping across the snowy plains with an icy wind fresh in her face. The song swelled to a climax. Ella was filled with immense happiness then, like a wave crashing down, the music ended, the pictures of the caribou fading away with the last notes.

Ella shuddered and took a deep breath. The caribou lowered its head, breaking eye contact. Ella gasped – its wound had miraculously healed! All that remained was a thin line of congealed blood and a few tufts of matted fur stuck to its chest. The caribou dipped its head, giving Ella the strong impression it was saying thank you, then, softly snorting, it trotted away. Ella watched it go, slumped against the bow rail, keeping her eyes on its bobbing figure until it caught up with the back of the herd. Then she relaxed and tried to remember what had happened. She wasn't exactly sure, but a faint fizzing feeling deep inside convinced her that magic had been at work. Elated but exhausted, Ella sat where she was until Blue twisted round in his harness.

"That was amazing!" he whispered, nudging her foot with his nose. "You were brilliant."

Ella smiled her thanks to Blue, and, pulling herself together, got off the sled.

"Well done," said Acer, thumping his tail in the snow. "Healing magic is very strong and takes practice to get right. For a first time that was impressive."

"Thank you." Ella knew she was blushing.

"Get on the sled as a passenger and we'll take you back," said Acer.

Ella wanted to protest that she was fit enough to drive, but standing was a bigger effort than it should have been, so she gave in gracefully. Sitting on the sled, her eyes felt heavy and her head drowsy, but she was determined not to miss a second of her time in the magical land of snow. Ella forced herself to stay awake as the dogs walked back down the hill.

"Who shot the caribou?" she called to Acer. "Do you know?"

"Someone who shoots for fun, not a local who hunts out of need," he answered. "Local people need caribou for their meat and fur. They shoot to kill. They'd never leave an injured animal to a painful death or as easy prey for a wolf."

"Wolves!" exclaimed Ella under her breath. It was easy to forget how many dangerous animals lived here when the landscape was so pretty.

"Wolves are shy creatures," said Acer kindly. "They rarely attack humans."

Reassured, Ella's thoughts turned to the mining company. They weren't local. Was it possible that one of their people had shot at the caribou for fun? Ella was sure that must be the answer or she wouldn't have been brought here to help. In the distance she could see Port Nanuk and she hoped that Acer was taking her to see Saskia before she went home. As they drew closer to the town Ella realised someone was sculpting a tall structure in the snow. Acer suddenly sped up, taking the dog team from a gentle jog to a run. Ella held on tight as the sled bounced across the snow. It was brilliant fun and she forgot about identifying the snow sculptor until they drew nearer. Even though Ella wasn't driving she could feel when Acer and Honey slowed the pace. The other dogs responded immediately and Ella guessed that

Acer was planning to draw up alongside the person building the enormous snowman. Curiously she leant forward half recognising the navy blue parka. A memory stirred in Ella's head, and just as she realised it was Jak, the sled hit a bump. Bandit slid right, pulling Coda with him. Coda's paws slipped and he frantically righted himself, but the movement sent the sled skittering on the snow.

"Help!" squeaked Ella, scared that they were about to run into Jak and the snowman he was building.

Feeling the sled was out of control, Acer and Honey veered to the left to correct it. Ella leant back against the bow rail, hoping her weight would help to slow them down. Blue and Inca pushed their paws firmly in the ground as they came to a wonky halt. The sled slid this way and that before slamming sideways into Jak's snowman. Freezing snow rained down on Ella, somehow finding its way down her neck.

"Eek!" she exclaimed, as something hard banged her arm.

Ella was so upset at crashing into Jak's snowman she was too shocked to speak. Jak had plenty to say.

"Watch where you're going," he shouted in a strong Canadian accent.

"I'm sorry." Ella was about to add that it wasn't her fault, but stopped. She was leader of the Starlight Snowdogs so she was responsible for any damage they caused.

"Sorry!" shouted Jak. "Sorry isn't good enough. It's taken me ages to build this. There isn't time to start again, it's nearly tea time."

He marched over to Ella and she shrank back, thinking he was going to hit her. Jak glared at her scornfully.

"I don't hit people, especially not girls."

Reaching out, he lifted up a wooden sign that had struck Ella when she'd crashed. A message was painted in wonky black letters across the centre. As Jak swung it over his shoulder Ella read the words:

"SAY NO TO MINING!"

"You're protesting about the diamond

drillers?" asked Ella, suddenly realising that Jak had built such an enormous snowman to hold his sign.

"Yes, I am," spat Jak. "We don't want *strangers* round here ruining things."

Chapter 9

Ella felt awful as Jak strode away. He must have spent ages building the snowman to protest about the mining company and in seconds it had been wrecked.

The dogs fidgeted restlessly and Ella realised she'd forgotten to give them the command to stand down from the sled.

"Free," she called hurriedly.

Scooping up a handful of snow, Ella started to rebuild the snowman. After a while Blue, Inca and Coda helped; rolling snowballs with their noses, they pushed them into a pile. Acer and Honey sat in the snow grooming their fur, and Bandit moved a short distance from the group, smugly watching. Ella pretended not to notice, but she wished she knew why Jak and Bandit disliked her so much.

Soon Ella noticed a group of people heading her way. As they drew closer she saw they were teenagers and one was riding a snowmobile. The driver was showing off and his antics got him stuck in a snowdrift. He stood up, leaning forward while revving the engine to pull the snowmobile free. His friends laughed and pelted him with snowballs. The group quickly divided themselves into two halves for a huge snowball fight. The snowmobile driver jumped down and joined them. There was a lot of laughter and good-natured shouting until finally a truce was called. Everyone helped push the snowmobile out of the snow, then they took it in turns to ride it home. Ella felt a pang of loneliness as they headed back to town. It would be fun to have a friend here, someone to have snowball fights with, share secrets and build snowmen. Sighing wistfully she went back to her work until something nudged at her hand. Looking down she saw it was Blue.

"Don't be sad," he whispered. "It's not your fault."

"I feel like it is," said Ella, stroking the top of Blue's head.

Blue half closed his eyes with pleasure as Ella continued to stroke him.

"I didn't mean to crash into Jak's snowman."

"That's not why he's upset," said Blue.

Ella's heart missed a beat. Did Blue know why Jak disliked her so much? She was going to ask him to explain, but as she formed her question Acer padded over, followed by Honey.

"It's time to go. It getting late," said Acer.

"But..." Ella was desperate to talk to Blue, but he was already hurrying back to the sled. An orangey pink sun was setting behind the

outline of Port Nanuk. Now she'd stopped working Ella noticed how cold it was. She shivered and shuffled her feet to warm her frozen toes. The teenagers had disappeared and she and the Starlight Snowdogs were totally alone in the icy landscape.

"It's not finished," she said, sadly sizing up the snowman.

"It'll still be here tomorrow," said Honey, kindly.

Ella smiled bravely. She might not be, though, and she'd wanted to finish the snowman for Jak, as a peace offering.

Blue was waiting for her in his harness. The remaining Starlight Snowdogs lined up alongside the sled to say goodbye. Inca rolled on her back and Ella scratched her tummy. Coda licked Ella's gloved hand and Honey rubbed her head against Ella's leg. Acer cocked his head for her to scratch behind his ears. Only Bandit sat stiffly, not moving a muscle as Ella stroked him.

"Bye, Bandit," she said softly.

The moment Ella sat on the sled, Blue started running across the snow in the opposite direction to Port Nanuk. Ella leant forward, hoping to talk to Blue before he took off, but Inca ran alongside the sled barking goodbye. Smothering her frustration, Ella waved at her.

"See you soon," she called, hoping that it was true.

The sled was moving so fast that everything blurred as it lifted into the air. Ella fell back against the driving bow and her stomach dipped then fluttered with excitement. Beneath her the dogs shrank to tiny black dots. It was freezing cold. Ella huddled deeper in her coat, wrapping her arms round her to keep warm. There was a sudden flash of green, then the sky went black. Ella closed her eyes, enjoying the swooping sensation as Blue towed her through the sky. She didn't normally feel this tired, but it had been an exciting visit. Healing the caribou had been incredible. Ella hoped that now the herd would reach its migration ground safely.

"We're going down!" Blue's sudden bark startled Ella.

"Great," she said, pulling herself back to the present.

Blue dropped steadily downwards until with a small jolt they landed. Ella fell on to her bottom, but Blue nudged her to her feet.

"Thanks," said Ella, hugging him.

"Thanks for what?" asked Mum, coming down the garden towards her.

Ella flushed.

"Thanks for being my puppy," she bluffed. "Where did you spring from?"

"I was about to ask you the same thing," Mum laughed. "I've been calling you to ask if you wanted a drink. Do you?"

"Yes, please," said Ella, then hurriedly changing the subject she asked, "How was your day?"

*   *   *

The week flew by and soon it was the weekend. On Saturday morning Ella woke early from a vivid dream where Saskia had been teaching her Inuit throat singing. They were in Saskia's kitchen and the dream was so real that Ella could smell chocolate fudge brownies baking in the oven. She was hopeless at the throat singing and couldn't get the breathing right. Saskia was very patient until Jak came in from the yard with Bandit.

"You're rubbish," he yelled. "You shouldn't be the leader of the Starlight Snowdogs."

It was only a dream, but Ella couldn't forget it and her heart hammered at the unpleasant words. She lay in bed with the duvet pulled over her nose while she reassured herself it wasn't real. After a while she felt better, but she couldn't help thinking that it would be fun to learn throat singing. Maybe it would help her the next time she found an injured arctic animal that needed healing. The more Ella thought about it the more excited she became with her idea. Leaping out of bed she switched on her computer and, sitting down in front of it, she waited impatiently for it to boot up. Ella felt a little guilty connecting to the Internet. She was supposed to ask first and tell her parents which website she was visiting. But it was far too early to wake them and she knew how to stay Internet safe. When the homepage finished loading Ella typed 'Inuit throat singing' into the search bar.

"Wow!" she said, her eyes widening as she stared at the screen.

There were lots of results and most of them were for *YouTube*. Ella's hand hovered over the mouse. Should she go on the site without asking? Ella's parents trusted her and she didn't want to break that trust. Suddenly she had an idea. Ella got up and opened the bedroom door. Now everyone could see what she was doing and if anyone woke up and asked about it then she would say it was for a school project.

Ella clicked on the first link and was taken to a black television screen. She hit the Play button and two women wearing long, white hooded robes appeared. They stood facing each other while holding on to their partner's elbows. The singing started and was so familiar it gave Ella goose bumps. With mounting excitement she played the video through twice. The rhythmic, breathless chanting sounded so simple, Ella was sure she could do it. Abandoning the computer she stood in the middle of her room and, clutching an imaginary partner, she took a deep breath. Immediately Saskia's words filled her head.

"You breathe in on the high notes and out on the deep ones."

Ella breathed in and made a high-pitched gasping sound, then huffing out her breath, she made a much deeper noise. But when she tried to breathe in again she couldn't make a sound and when she exhaled the sound came

out too high. Giggling at the awful noise she was making, Ella tried again. It took her a while to co-ordinate sounds and breathing, but at last she managed to get a rhythm with the two notes. It didn't sound anything like the women on YouTube, or the wonderful singing she'd heard in her head the day she'd healed the caribou, but Ella was cheered by her efforts and was thoroughly enjoying herself. She jumped a mile when a pyjama-clad Daisy burst through the bedroom door.

"Ella, is everything OK? Are you ill? Shall I get Mum?"

Chapter 10

Ella's face flamed with embarrassment.

"It's for school," she stuttered. "It's a type of singing."

Daisy looked at her blankly.

"For school?" she repeated.

"Erm, yeah. It's music from around the world," Ella improvised. "I've chosen—"

Daisy held up a hand, cutting Ella off.

"Let me get this right," she said, her voice squeaky with indignation. "At half-past six on a Saturday morning you are practising a song for school?"

Ella opened her mouth to reply, but Daisy was on a roll.

"Do you know how hard I'm working right now? I've got exams at school and a big ice-skating competition coming up. I need my sleep, Ella. I'm surprised at your selfishness."

"I'm sorry, I didn't mean to wake you up." Ella was embarrassed and upset.

"Well, don't do it again," said Daisy huffily, backing out of the room.

Ella felt deflated. She couldn't carry on with her singing, but she was too awake to go

back to bed. Deciding to go down and see Blue, she switched off her computer and dressed in a long-sleeved top and her favourite trousers. At least Blue was pleased to see her. He squeaked with delight, rolling on to his back and waving his paws in the air as Ella scratched his furry tummy.

"You'd have me do that all day, wouldn't you?" asked Ella, breaking off to get Blue a dog treat.

Her stomach rumbled hungrily and Ella decided not to wait for everyone else but to get her own breakfast. She was digging around in the cupboard for her favourite cereal when she heard the letterbox rattle. The postman was early today! Ella found the cornflakes and turned to put them on the table, when something whizzed past her and out into the hall.

"Blue!" called Ella, dropping the cereal box on the table. "Come back."

But it was too late. Blue was already at the door and judging from his muffled growls he was helping the post through the letterbox.

"Blue, leave!" said Ella, running after him.

By the time she reached the door, Blue had helped the mail inside and was proudly standing over it. Ella groaned. Two letters and a packet, all punctured with teeth marks, lay on the floor.

"Oh, Blue," said Ella, picking them up. "I hope it's not anything important."

The packet was addressed to Miss Daisy Edwards. Ella's heart missed a beat as she turned it over.

"No!" she whispered. "Please don't let this be what I think it is."

But there was no doubt about it. The squashy package had a sender's name and address on the back. Ice Dancers Ltd, Palace Road, Birmingham.

A feeling of doom swept over Ella as she inspected the damage. There were three holes; silky red material poked through two of them and a gold sequin through the third. Blue's teeth had punctured the material and one of the sequins was hanging off. A door opened upstairs. With a thudding heart Ella raced to the kitchen and shoved the letters and the packet containing Daisy's new competition skate dress inside. Her hands were trembling as she slammed the drawer shut. Whatever was she going to say to Daisy? An apology wouldn't be enough. When she saw her dress Daisy was going to explode!

Ella hoped that Mum would come down to breakfast first so she could explain what had happened, but Daisy beat her by a few seconds. It was so typical. The one morning Ella wanted a quiet moment with Mum there was never the right opportunity. Daisy dawdled over breakfast, cupping her hands round her mug of tea and sleepily staring into space.

"What time does the postman come?" asked Dad, who always missed him on a week day as he'd left for work. "I'm waiting for an important letter from my accountant."

Ella stared at Dad in disbelief. Was there no end to her problems? What if Dad's letter had come today?

"And I'm waiting for my skate dress," said Daisy. "The competition's in two weeks' time and I need to practise in it. It should be here today. We paid for first class post."

Ella took a deep breath. There was never a good time to break bad news so she might as well get it over with.

"I've got something to tell you," she said quietly.

Ella had expected Daisy to be angry, but what happened next was worse. After she'd finished explaining and apologising, and handing out the bitten post, Daisy burst into tears.

"Don't cry, love," soothed Mum. "It might not be as bad as you think."

Deftly she opened the parcel. The skate dress was wrapped in a clear plastic bag and, pulling it out, Mum held it up. It was suddenly very quiet in the kitchen. Ella held her breath. The silence was broken by Daisy.

"No," she screamed, dramatically slumping across the table and burying her head in her arms.

Mum looked sideways at the dress and

took a sharp intake of breath. Ella could hardly bear to look, but forced herself to examine it too. It was worse than she'd hoped. There was a hole just below the neckline right in the centre of the dress and another on the hip and several gold sequins were hanging on by a thread. The material was so fine that even the pressure of holding it up was making the holes run like laddered tights. Quickly, Mum hung the dress over the back of a chair to stop the holes from getting any bigger.

"Oh, Blue!" she said.

Ella didn't dare ask Dad if the letter he was opening was the important one he was expecting.

"I'm sorry," she gabbled. "It wasn't Blue's

fault. It was mine. Blame me for leaving the door open. I'm responsible for Blue getting at the post."

"Ella," said Mum in a tight voice. "Just make yourself scarce. And take Blue with you."

Ella didn't need to be told twice. Grabbing Blue by the collar she led him out into the garden.

"We'll go to my den," she said, pulling a startled Blue towards the brightly painted caravan at the end of the garden.

The caravan was stuffy inside so Ella opened the windows, knocking a few dead flies into the garden in the process. The pretty green and yellow curtains fluttered in the

autumn breeze. Ella took a deep breath of the fresh morning air then slumped down on the bean bag, pulling Blue with her.

"You've done it now!" she whimpered. "You're still on trial. What if Mum and Dad decide you have to go? Competition dresses cost a fortune. Mum can't afford another one."

Blue licked Ella's face then wriggled to go free.

Ella hugged him tightly then reluctantly let him go.

Unaware he was in disgrace, Blue nosed around the den, sniffing at everything. Eventually he settled down and, resting his head in between his front paws, he fell asleep.

Ella couldn't settle. She wanted to go round to Isabel's. Her friend always made her feel better when she had a problem. But Blue couldn't go for walks until he'd completed a full course of vaccinations and after this morning's antics Ella didn't dare leave him alone. She searched the bookcase for something to read, but nothing appealed. Then she had a brainwave. Pulling out her colouring pencils and a sheet of paper Ella set about making Daisy a card to say she was sorry.

Ella spent ages on the card. It wouldn't fix Daisy's dress, but it might make her feel better if she knew how sorry Ella felt about it. When the card was finished she used another sheet of paper to make an envelope and decorated it with pictures of Daisy's ice-skating boots and her flute. Deciding she'd made herself scarce for long enough, Ella put away the colouring pencils then woke the sleepy Blue.

"Come on, you," she said. "It's time to say sorry."

Unsure of the reception she'd get, Ella carried Blue back to the house. In the short time she'd had Blue he'd already grown.

"You're getting a fatty," she teased him, as she staggered towards the door. "I won't be able to lift you soon."

Ella didn't think she'd be able to open the back door and hold Blue without crushing

Daisy's card, so she stopped to put him down. As she lowered him on to the back-door step she heard Mum and Dad in the kitchen, talking in low voices. Ella didn't mean to eavesdrop, but hearing Blue's name she hesitated.

"I agree it's serious," said Mum. "So what do you want to do about it?"

Ella felt as if someone had thrown her into the icy river near Port Nanuk. "It wasn't your fault," she whispered to Blue fiercely. "It was mine. I shouldn't have left the door open. They've got to give you another chance."

But what if Mum and Dad didn't? What would happen to Blue? And who would lead the Starlight Snowdogs?

Ella went to open the door, determined to plead Blue's case, but as she reached out to open it she heard the distant howl of dogs. Blue tensed, then wriggling madly, tried to jump out of Ella's arms. The dogs howled again, sending shivers skittering along Ella's spine. Propping Daisy's card against the back door, Ella put Blue down and, clutching his collar, fled down the garden with him.

Chapter 11

Blue was heading straight for Dad's vegetable patch and Ella somehow managed to pull him to one side. They streaked across the lawn and the moment Blue leapt into the air Ella jumped with him. Up they flew into the bright autumn sky, leaving behind the houses and gardens and the toy-sized roads with the dinky cars and buses beetling along them.

Without warning the sky changed from clear blue to coal black. It was freezing cold and Ella gritted her teeth, screwing up her eyes against the piercing wind. She could smell snow and soon she flew into a blizzard. The snowflakes whirled around her, stinging her hands and face like icy bees.

"Blue!" shrieked Ella, when the wind ripped him away from her.

She hadn't meant to shout. Nothing bad would happen to him, but after the morning's events Ella couldn't help herself. Ashamed of her outburst she spread her arms, relaxing into the wind and letting it carry her like the snowflakes. As she relaxed she began to enjoy herself and it was a little disappointing to feel the sled appear beneath her. But the sled ride was even more brilliant. Ella held up her arms, lapping up the magical starlight that made her feel fizzy inside. Blue was enjoying it too and carried his tail proudly over his back. Away in the distance Ella saw the faint tinge of coloured lights. Rapidly they spun closer, wrapping Ella in green and purple ribbons then, stretching out across the sky, they changed colour from pink to white, and purple to green. It was a fantastic display and Ella was sorry when the lights faded away to nothing. Suddenly she was dazzled by a flash of green that illuminated the whole sky. It was accompanied by purple streaks like coloured rain. The sled dropped and the ground rushed closer. Blue landed neatly, stopping in a few long strides with his ears pricked and his plumed tail arched. It was snowing heavily. Ella wiped the snow from her snow goggles as she climbed off the sled and waited with Blue for the Starlight Snowdogs to arrive.

Seconds later she saw them. Snow sprayed from their paws as they raced closer. Acer was in the lead with Honey second, followed by Bandit, Coda and Inca bringing up the rear. Acer came to a neat halt a paw's length from Ella. Honey stopped with her usual grace, but Inca and Coda collided with each other and nearly landed on their noses. Bandit gave a grumpy growl as they bumped into him.

"Welcome," panted Acer. "We have a serious problem."

"What's wrong?" asked Ella, noticing how quickly the dogs took up their places on the gangline.

"The mining company has been using a helicopter. It's spooked the migrating caribou and the herd is running the wrong way. They're heading straight for a ravine. You have to stop them!"

Ella felt hot then cold. If the herd ran over the edge of the ravine there would be terrible injuries, and deaths. There wasn't a second to waste. With trembling hands she ran down the gangline checking the dogs. Satisfied everything was in order, she jumped on to the back of the sled and, leaning over the driving bow, shouted, "Hike!"

The sled jolted as the dogs leapt away, their paws sinking in the fresh snow. With outstretched necks they battled on. Ella leant forward, yelling encouragement at them. It was snowing so fast she could hardly see where she was going. Time and again she bent her head to wipe the snow on her goggles away with her arm. An icy wind whipped her face and Ella was grateful for the huge fur-lined hood to keep her head and ears warm. The sled bumped and jolted on, going so fast that Ella had no time to work out where they were or where they were heading. Her hands grew stiff from clutching the gangline and her legs ached with the effort of riding the bumps. But even in her discomfort it was an exhilarating ride and knowing the caribou were in such danger, Ella urged the dogs to go faster. A short while later she noticed multiple animal prints in the snow.

Caribou!

Acer's ears twitched. Ella listened, then she heard it too. In the distance a faint thudding noise. Acer ran even faster and Ella glanced worriedly at Blue and Inca. They were only trainees. Would they keep up? The smaller dogs were giving their all. Ears pricked forward, tails high over their backs, they bravely galloped on, but they were working much harder than the older dogs.

Their sides were heaving and their breath rose in thick white clouds. The thudding grew steadily louder until Ella could see a handful of caribou galloping ahead. These were the stragglers.

"Haw," called Ella, shifting her weight with the dogs as they obediently turned to the left.

She drove the sled in a wide arc to overtake the back of the herd. The noise was deafening. Ella insides trembled. The herd was out of control, their hooves pounding in the snow as they ran with heads high and parallel to the ground, and their tails pointed stiffly upwards. She had to get control of the herd and lead it away from the ravine – but how? One false move and the Starlight Snowdogs would be trampled as the spooked caribou charged on. At first Ella was so scared she could hardly think, but she forced herself to remain calm and, as her thoughts cleared, she was conscious of a wonderful feeling growing inside her. It was like having a friendly swarm of bees buzzing round her body. The buzzing swelled like a wave, lifting Ella and filling her with confidence. From nowhere a series of images ran through her head, the pictures showing Ella ways of helping the caribou. Suddenly Ella was so excited she wanted to shout for joy. She could do this. The magic was helping her to make the right decisions.

Inca stumbled, snapping Ella out of her dream. She held her breath, willing Blue's sister not to fall. Inca quickly recovered her footing, but her tail drooped and Ella could see she was shaken. Blue was flagging too. His breath was laboured and his sides were heaving. Despite the urgency of the situation, Ella felt her mind clear and somehow, instinctively, she knew what must be done. It required a new skill, but Ella was sure she could master it. Taking a deep breath she cleared her mind and focused on her task.

Chapter 12

For a moment Ella gave Acer total control of the sled so she could concentrate on Inca and Blue. She wiped her goggles again. It was snowing heavily and she had to squint to make out the tuglines. Her gaze followed the ropes from where they joined the gangline to each dog's harness.

"Free," murmured Ella, her eyes boring

first into Blue and then Inca's harness.

She imagined the harnesses falling away, allowing the dogs to run free. As she concentrated, a warm tingling feeling like an electrical current passed through her whole body. There was a hissing noise in her ears. Ella stared at the harnesses, willing them undone, then suddenly the leather opened and Blue and Inca dived sideways, running clear of the sled. They dropped back until they were running alongside Ella, Inca having dipped behind the sled so she was the same side as Blue.

"I need you to go ahead," Ella shouted. "Overtake the herd and head them off from the ravine."

"We're on it," barked Blue.

Inca waved her tail and the two dogs accelerated away, faster now they'd shed their load and were running free. Soon they disappeared in the falling snow.

Ella drove the remaining snowdogs on, steadily making her way to the front of the herd. It was an amazing feeling to run with the caribou – exhilarating yet terrifying. The sled was so close that by reaching out Ella could have touched their hairy bodies. Snow flicked up from the caribous' hooves into Ella's face. But running with the caribou wasn't enough. To stop the herd from falling into the ravine Ella had to turn them. It was a dangerous, almost impossible, task, but there was no other option. Slowly Ella counted down from three.

"Gee," she yelled, and sucking in her breath, she steered the snowdogs into the caribou. The noise was tremendous. Ella was conscious that she was up against the full might of the herd. Legs and hooves thundered so close to her that one slip and— Ella stamped on the thought, refusing to let the danger scare her. She drove the sled closer, marvelling at the dogs who obeyed her command, running into the caribou without a second's hesitation. Ella could feel the steamy warmth of sweating caribou and smell their musky animal odour. For several tense seconds Ella and the herd ran neck and neck. Heart racing and hands sweating inside her gloves, Ella held her ground, conscious that if the herd didn't move over she would run the Starlight Snowdogs over the ravine with them. Then gradually the caribou began to turn. Ella pressed home her advantage, forcing them away from the deadly ravine.

Blue and Inca were ahead, solidly standing in the original path of the fleeing herd. But the caribou were already turning and Blue and Inca were no longer in danger of being mown down. One or two stray caribou didn't turn in time, but Blue and Inca were ready for them, guiding them back to the herd with a sharp howl. The sled drew closer then tore past. Ella nodded, but Blue and Inca were too busy concentrating to acknowledge her back.

Finally Ella slowed the pace, letting the herd slip past her until a very long while later there were only the stragglers left.

When the last caribou had gone Ella halted the dogs.

"Whoa, and free," she shouted joyfully, leaping from the sled. "Well done, everyone. We did it!"

Blue gave Ella a swift lick on the face before joining the other dogs rolling together on the ground.

It had stopped snowing, but there was something in the air that sparkled like diamonds as it fell.

"What is it?" asked Ella.

"Diamond dust," said Acer. "It's when the

moisture in the air freezes and falls as ice."

"It's pretty." Ella held out her arms so the diamond dust could fall on her.

There was so much beauty in the natural world. Ella wished that people could enjoy it where it was without feeling the need to own it. The promise of a diamond in a ring or a necklace had nearly caused the loss of a herd of caribou. It made no sense. Sighing wistfully, Ella watched the dogs roll ecstatically in the snow. Minutes later they were joined by Blue and Inca.

"Couldn't keep up?" said Bandit scornfully.

Ella ran over, her boots making deep prints in the fresh snow.

"You were brilliant," she said, wrapping an

arm round each dog's neck and hugging them tightly to her. "We couldn't have done it without you."

"Thank you," panted Inca, licking Ella's hand, while Blue jumped up and, sticking his nose in Ella's collar, licked her on the ear.

"Eww!" she squealed. Giggling, she pushed him off, then, scooping up a handful of snow, she balled and threw it.

Snap! Blue caught the snowball in his mouth. It disintegrated in a flurry of white flakes. Ella rolled more snowballs, tossing them high in the air as fast as she could for Blue, Inca and Coda to chase.

"Catch," said Ella, throwing a snowball at Bandit.

He caught it and Ella laughed, guessing from the expression on his face that his response was instinctive and he hadn't meant to.

"Come on, Bandit, just this once. Play snowballs with me," Ella begged.

Bandit ignored her and slunk behind the sled, lying down in the snow so she couldn't see him.

"I'll play," said Honey, getting to her paws.

It was a riotous game. Ella had a tough time keeping up with the four dogs, especially Coda, who wasn't so agile, but was extremely good at catching snowballs.

After a while Ella called an end to the game and flopped down on the sled for a rest. Inca and Blue snuffled in the snow, digging tracks with their noses, but eventually they settled down together, basking in the weak autumn sunshine.

It was incredibly quiet. Ella had never appreciated how wonderful silence could sound. The noise of nothing filled her with happiness as she admired the ice-white landscape, until something rustled nearby. Swivelling round, Ella caught her breath as an arctic hare hopped from underneath a snow-clad bush. The hare was pure white with long, black-tipped ears. It sat up on its hind legs, whiskers twitching, as it sampled the air. Ella sat totally still, not daring to move. The hare's nose was working overtime. Sensing Ella and the dogs, it turned its head and fixed the group with an unblinking stare. Then away it streaked across the snow, covering the ground in long, agile bounds.

Ella sighed. Acer stood up and, stretching gracefully, he padded over.

"You did a good job with the caribou," he complimented her.

Ella hesitated.

"Thanks," she said eventually.

Acer laid his head in her lap.

"What's wrong?"

"I don't know. I'm probably being silly, but I have a feeling that it's not over. The caribou aren't safe yet." Ella hardly dared look at Acer, fearing she'd embarrassed herself.

"Instinct shouldn't be ignored," said Acer simply. "What are you going to do about it?"

Ella hesitated.

"Go after the herd?" she suggested.

"Good," said Acer. "Let's get going."

Ella felt guilty getting the dogs back into their harnesses when they'd worked so hard, but only Bandit complained. Ella had the strong impression his protests were more for the sake of it rather than because he didn't want to go on another expedition. His lack of co-operation irritated her, though, and she suddenly snapped, "Are you a Starlight Snowdog or not?"

That shocked him. It shocked Ella too. Why had she let Bandit get to her like that?

But her loss of control wasn't such a bad thing.

"I am," said Bandit stiffly, and without any more fuss he took up his place in the line.

Acer said nothing, but Ella knew from the set of his head that he approved. Gathering up the gangline, she sent the dogs forward.

Chapter 13

The caribou had left a clear trail in the freshly fallen snow for Ella and the Starlight Snowdogs to follow. Keeping her eyes to the ground, Ella steered the sled after the broad hoof marks. The dazzling white landscape was dotted with small, snow-covered bushes and single trees. The land undulated, sometimes sloping upwards and at other times falling away beneath them. Ella kept the dogs running at a smart trot and after a long while they caught sight of the back of the caribou herd.

"Hike," cried Ella, urging the dogs to go faster.

Unaware of their presence, the caribou peacefully ambled along and soon Ella caught them up. Not wanting to spook the herd again, she gave the stragglers a wide berth as she pushed the dogs on by. The herd seemed content enough, but Ella wasn't satisfied. Something was urging her on and she kept going until she'd overtaken them. Soon she recognised some of the landscape – the three trees leaning together like gossiping friends and the impressive coniferous tree with the Y-shaped fork. Then Ella noticed the dogs were behaving strangely, tossing their heads and sniffing the air.

"What is it?" she called to Acer.

"People ahead," he barked. "A large group."

Ella leant forward, straining her eyes to see until, sledging over a ridge in the snow, she saw a crowd of people in the distance. She called to the dogs to slow. What was going on? Why had so many people gathered here? The crowd was made up of both the young and old and most people were dressed in parkas with huge, fur-lined hoods. Many were carrying banners. Ella was too far away to read what the protest was about, but she could guess.

Behind the crowd lay the pine forest where the diamond team were drilling. As she drew nearer she saw that the protesters had spread themselves out in a long line across the snow. Ella was surprised and impressed at the size of the group. There had to be several hundred people. But they couldn't protest here, not now, when the herd of migrating caribou were coming this way. The protestors' well-meaning actions were going to endanger the animals they were trying to protect. Ella had to get them to move, but how? It was an enormous task for one person, even with the Starlight Snowdogs.

Sensing her hesitation, the dogs slowed, but Ella pushed them on again. She might not have a plan, but there was no time to waste. The caribou would be here soon. Muddled thoughts rushed round her head, then suddenly she remembered something. Jak! He'd been building a snowman to protest about the mining company. Maybe he was here today too.

"Bandit," called Ella. "Is Jak here?"

For a second Ella thought that Bandit might not answer, but she'd underestimated him.

"Yes," he said, a trifle grudgingly.

"Wait here," she instructed the dogs, "I need to find him."

Jak had a round face and jet-black hair, thought Ella, conjuring up a picture of him. He also wore a navy blue parka. Ella scanned the crowd. There were so many people in blue parkas. Was that him over there? Ella hurried over, but as she drew nearer, the person turned and Ella saw it was a girl. Disappointed, she continued searching, but it was like looking for a snowflake in a snowdrift. Time was running out. Ella took long, slow breaths, determined to stay calm. There had to be an easier way of finding Jak. Then suddenly she had it. She raced back to the sled.

"Bandit, I need your help," she burst out.

Bandit ignored Ella, but she ploughed on.

"Bandit, please, can you find Jak for me?"

Any of the Starlight Snowdogs could track Jak by his scent, but as Bandit was Jak's dog, it was right to ask him first. There was a long

silence and Ella could sense the other dogs'
impatience. Then suddenly Bandit spoke.

"Let me go free," he growled.

"Free," said Ella.

As the harness dropped away Bandit sprang
forward, his nose sniffing at the snow.
Trembling with relief Ella followed him as he
quickly wove through the crowd. There were
so many people here. Would Bandit be able to
fix on to Jak's scent? Suddenly Bandit sped up.
Ella hurried after him, her face shining with
relief as she spotted Jak standing by a tree,
fiddling with a banner on a long pole. As Ella
drew nearer, Jak looked up, smiling in
surprise at Bandit. Ella seemed to baffle him,
as if he couldn't work out why she was here.

Then suddenly remembering, he scowled fiercely and turned away.

Ella's hopes were instantly dashed. Why ever had she thought Jak would help when he'd made it clear that he didn't like her? Helplessly, Ella stared at the crowd. There was only one thing for it. She would have to move the people on her own. But where should she start? She walked towards a teenage girl, planning what she would say, but the girl was chatting to a friend and Ella felt silly interrupting. What if the girl didn't believe her? A sudden flash of anger surged through Ella. Jak was her only hope. If he was serious about protecting the environment, then he had to help. Breathing deeply, Ella turned back and approached him.

"Hello, Jak," she said boldly, hiding her hands behind her back so that he couldn't see how they were trembling.

"Hello," he grunted.

"You've got to help me." Ella didn't mean to blurt out her request so bluntly, but once she'd started she couldn't stop. The words tumbled out of their own accord. Jak listened silently and when she'd finished he said, "I'll help. This is what we'll do."

Jak recruited the help of his many friends and with each of them spreading the word, it didn't take long before the crowd started to move. The effect was like sand trickling through an hourglass. Once a few people shifted, the crowd slowly followed. Jak and Ella walked faster, leading the protestors a good distance away from the path they expected the caribou to take. Then in the distance Ella saw the first caribou. A silence fell as the approaching animal trotted closer. Ella's stomach flip-flopped. Even now the sight of so many animals was thrilling. A smile spread over her face as the dense herd of caribou, their magnificent antlers bobbing up and down, surged closer.

Suddenly there was movement in the crowd and a small child slipped from the group and tottered across the snow.

"No!" gasped Ella.

The toddler was unaware of the caribou pounding towards him and stood in the path of the oncoming charge. Without thinking Ella

dashed across the snow. The child's mother suddenly noticed what was happening and let out a high-pitched scream. It spooked the caribou, and the leading animals broke into a run. Ella panicked. What should she do? Could she use her magic to rescue the child? No! With a sinking heart she realised her magic couldn't help in this situation. She was on her own. Ella felt like she was watching the scene play out on television and that it wasn't her legs propelling her forward. Or her arms that reached up and scooped the baby out of the path of the oncoming caribou. The baby was heavy and struggled with fright. Ella gripped him tighter and ran as fast as she could out of the way. A nanosecond later the

ground where the child had stood was engulfed by the stampeding animals.

The mother ran to Ella, plucking the baby out of her arms with tearful thanks. Willingly Ella handed him over and, not wanting a fuss, melted into the crowd. As the caribou realised there was no threat, they slowed up. Ella watched them for a bit, but the herd would take ages to pass through. Her work was done here. She hurried back to the dogs and found them still in harness as they patiently waited for her to return.

"Well done," said Acer. "That was excellent and very brave."

"Jak helped. I couldn't have done it without him," said Ella, and Bandit, who'd come up behind her, thumped his tail in approval.

It was time to go home. Reluctantly Ella said her goodbyes, releasing all of the dogs from the harnesses except for Blue. Inca covered her in licks and even Bandit grudgingly nudged her leg when she gave him a goodbye stroke. Ella climbed on the sled, grateful that this time she was a passenger.

"OK, Blue," she called. "Home!"

"Yap!" barked Blue, but as he stepped out Ella heard a shout.

"Wait!"

She leant out of the sled to see who was calling and to her enormous surprise saw Jak running towards her.

Chapter 14

"**D**on't go!" Jak hurried closer, his feet crunching in the powder-soft snow.

"Whoa," said Ella, pulling Blue up.

She waited nervously as Jak came alongside the sled. He looked at Ella then quickly glanced away.

There was a long uncomfortable silence until Jak said gruffly, "Look, I'm sorry. I was mean to you; the snowball attack and being nasty when you crashed into my snowman."

"The snowballs! So that was you. But why?" asked Ella.

"It wasn't your fault. Well, it was sort of," Jak's face flushed with embarrassment.

Ella felt uncomfortable sitting on her own so she shifted up and patted the sled for him to join her. He hesitated then, plonking himself down, grunted, "Thanks."

Remembering the ferocity of the snowball attack Ella said quietly, "I didn't stand a chance."

Jak grimaced.

"I wasn't very nice. It's not an excuse but, well, it's because I was disappointed. I still am if

I'm honest. I thought I'd be chosen as the new leader of the Starlight Snowdogs. I couldn't believe it when you were picked instead."

"Oh!" Ella was lost for words. "I can't believe it's me either. You'd make a brilliant leader."

"No! It has to be you," said Jak passionately. "Especially after what you did today, going after that baby by yourself. The magic couldn't have helped you then. You were on your own."

"You would have done the same if you'd realised," said Ella.

Jak shrugged.

"You still make a better leader than me. I believe in magic and the legend of the Starlight Snowdogs, but it's not enough. I live here. You can do so much more than I can. You can spread the message further. You can show the people in your land how the way you live has an effect on our lives here."

"Saskia said the same thing," Ella remembered. "But what's the legend of the Starlight Snowdogs? She never told me that."

"Well," said Jak, shifting into a more comfortable position, "you know about the Northern Lights?"

"Er, no," Ella confessed.

"The Northern Lights are a natural light display that can sometimes be seen in polar regions at night time. They're amazing. The sky's lit with fantastic green lights and sometimes there are other colours too."

Ella nodded, excitedly realising she saw those lights each time she was brought to the Arctic.

As Jak talked, Bandit rested his head on Jak's lap. The Starlight Snowdogs gathered round and Blue slipped his harness to sit next to Ella.

"The story goes that late one night a hunter was returning home when he found a dog half buried in the snow. She'd given birth to a litter of puppies and all six of them had frozen to death. The hunter put the dog and her puppies on to his sled and took them home. On his way back, the Northern Lights, or Aurora Borealis as they're also called, gave an amazing light display. The dead pups were drenched in beautiful coloured lights and miraculously it revived them. The hunter nursed the dog back to health, along with her puppies, who grew to be big and strong. The hunter called the mother dog Aurora. Aurora was the most loyal dog the hunter had ever owned and her puppies were too. They took great care of him. One day when he was out on the ice, the dogs halted and refused to go any further. The hunter couldn't understand why the dogs had disobeyed him. When he investigated, he discovered that he had been riding towards a hidden ravine. The dogs had sensed it and by stopping had saved his life. But the dogs weren't just clever. Before long the hunter realised that they all had magical properties, which they used to help other animals. These dogs were the first ever Starlight Snowdogs. Eventually they died of old age, but all of them had puppies and the magic was passed on. It works the same as it does in humans. Only a few dogs can truly recognise the magic within them. These are the ones that go on to become the Starlight Snowdogs."

There was a long silence, then Ella said, "So the magic comes from the Northern Lights."

"Magic is all around us," said Jak. "The Northern Lights are part of that magic; it boosts what you already have inside you."

There was so much to take in. Ella loved the legend of the Starlight Snowdogs and wanted to fix it in her memory.

"So Bandit's your dog," she said at last.

"Yes." Lovingly Jak stroked the top of Bandit's head. "One of my biggest disappointments about not becoming the leader of the Starlight Snowdogs was not being able to talk to him."

"He seems to understand you."

Jak nodded.

"I understand him too."

"So what happens now? Do you still hate me, or do you think we might be friends?" asked Ella shyly.

"Friends," said Jak hesitantly.

"Good," said Ella. "And maybe we can help each other?"

"Maybe," Jak agreed.

Ella didn't expect for her and Jak to become instant best friends, but it was a start.

"Are you coming back to see my grandma?"

Ella would have loved to visit Saskia, especially now she'd formed a truce with Jak, but she knew she had to go home.

"I'd really like that, but I have to go," she said sadly.

"Next time then," said Jak, standing up.

"Definitely," Ella agreed.

As Jak moved away from the sled the dogs followed, sitting in a line as Ella and Blue prepared for their journey home. Blue, back in his harness, ran across the snowy ground and the dogs leapt up and followed, waving their tails and barking goodbye. Only Bandit remained where he was, by Jak's side. Ella didn't mind. She was sure his tail twitched as the sled whizzed past and that was a start too.

The sled raced across the snowy ground then gracefully shot upwards, leaving Ella breathless with the thrill of it. She hung over the side waving to Jak and the dogs as they shrank away to nothing. There was a sudden flash of green light tinged with pink at the edges, then darkness fell. Pushing her windswept hair from her face Ella leant against the driving bow and let Blue fly her home. It was a smooth ride and soon the sled began to descend. Earthwards they spiralled until Ella felt the sled fall away and she landed in the garden at a run. Blue landed next to her, neatly on all four paws.

"Wuff," he barked.

"Wuff, yourself," said Ella.

Ecstatically Blue rolled in the grass, ending up on his back with his front paws tucked up and his long pink tongue hanging out.

"You're mad," said Ella, squatting down to scratch his tummy.

Blue groaned with delight and thumped his tail on the ground.

It had been such an exciting time in the Arctic that it took Ella several minutes before she remembered her home life. But once she did it was like being engulfed in a damp grey cloud. Ella lay down beside Blue and her eyes filled with tears. Blue gazed back at her then, as if to say, "What's up?" he licked her on the nose.

Ella managed a weak smile.

"They can't send you away. Not now," she whispered fiercely. "They have to give you one more chance; I couldn't stand it if I had to give you up."

Chapter 15

The card Ella had made for Daisy was still propped against the back door and, picking it up, she went inside. Mum and Dad were sitting at the table with the ruined skate dress spread out between them. They stopped talking as Ella entered. Ella's eyes were drawn to the holes. They didn't look as bad as she'd remembered them, but the dress was definitely ruined. There was an awkward silence, then everyone spoke at once.

"It wasn't Blue's fault, it was mine," said Ella. "I'll pay for Daisy's dress out of my pocket money. It might take a while though."

"It wasn't Blue's fault," said Mum and Dad.

Ella was so desperate to take the blame away from Blue that it took a moment to work out what her parents were saying.

"S-so…" she stuttered eventually. "You're not blaming Blue then?"

"Blue's only a puppy," said Dad. "You have to teach him how to behave, Ella."

Ella's heart thudded loudly. Dad had made it clear that training Blue was her job. So what would happen now she'd failed? Would he

send Blue away? Ella steeled herself to ask when Daisy came into the kitchen. Her eyes were puffy and red and she was sniffing. At once Ella felt even worse. Daisy worked so hard at her ice skating, she didn't deserve this. The home-made card didn't seem enough to say sorry, but it was all she had. Hesitantly Ella held it out to her big sister. Daisy looked as if she was going to refuse to take it, but then reached out and slowly opened it. She stared at the card for a long time. Then, bending down, she stroked Blue's head.

"You're a bad puppy," she said sadly. "But I can't help liking you, even though you've spoilt my dress."

"It's not totally ruined," Mum interrupted.

"I can stop the material running by sewing a patch inside the dress and I could cover the holes with sequins. I'm sure we can buy extra ones from somewhere."

"Will it look all right?" asked Daisy. "It won't look stupid or anything?"

"Are you calling my sewing stupid?" asked Mum jokily.

Daisy gave a half smile.

"No, of course not. It's just…"

"The dress will look fantastic when I've finished with it," said Mum reassuringly. "Trust me."

Daisy sighed with relief.

"Thanks, Mum, and thanks for the card, Ella. And as for you…" Daisy couldn't help

giggling a little at Blue, who had rolled over so she could scratch his tummy.

"I never wanted a dog," said Dad suddenly. "Dogs are hard work."

Ella's chest tightened. Was Dad about to say that she couldn't keep Blue any more? Well, if that happened then she'd run away. Maybe she and Blue could go to Saskia's and live there? But deep down Ella knew she couldn't run away from home. She'd miss her family far too much and it wasn't like running away ever solved anything. Far better to face up to your problems and work out how to deal with them, than to have the problems go with you.

Ella threw her arms round Blue's neck and buried her face in his soft fur.

"I'll come and visit you," she whispered. "If they send you away I'll visit you every day."

"Ella, are you listening?" asked Dad.

Ella stood up and faced her father.

"I said that in a short time I've grown quite fond of this young scallywag. You're doing a great job with him, but it's not fair to expect you to train him all by yourself. So from now on I'm going to help you."

Ella was so surprised she thought she must have misheard.

"You're going to let Blue stay?"

"Yes," said Dad. "But we've all got to be more careful. Puppies are like small children. You have to keep a constant eye on them. It's up to everyone to remember to shut Blue in

the kitchen when the postman's due. Don't leave shoes and things lying around. And until Blue's old enough for puppy classes I'll teach him a few commands."

Ella could hardly believe her good luck. Her heart swooped with joy and she flung herself at Dad and hugged him tightly.

"Thanks, Dad."

"We'll start right now," said Dad. "Take Blue into the garden and I'll be out in a minute."

Ella didn't need to be told twice. Calling Blue to follow her, she hurried outside. The silky bantam hens were searching for worms in the grass. They eyed Blue suspiciously as he gambolled towards them.

"Don't even think about it," said Ella, grabbing Blue by the collar. Then remembering that wasn't a proper command she said firmly, "Blue, leave."

Blue strained against his collar, then realising Ella meant business, he stopped pulling and rubbed his head against her arm. A feeling like tiny electrical pulses tingled through Ella's fingers as she brushed them against Blue's snowflake dog tag. Catching hold of it she held it tightly. The snowflake was cold as ice and for a brief second Ella imagined herself in the Arctic, the icy air nipping her nose and making her cheeks glow. In the distance there was the faint howl of dogs. A butterfly flitted past and the image disappeared. Ella sighed happily. She couldn't wait for her next expedition. There was still so much for her to learn and now there was Jak to get to know too. But first there was work to do here.

"Blue, sit," she said. "Good boy."

See where it all began...

THE STARLIGHT SNOWDOGS

THE LAND OF SNOW

Skye Waters

Mum was watching from her office window and opened the front door before Ella could get her key out.

"You're late. I was beginning to worry—" she broke off, suddenly noticing the sleeping puppy. "Oh, how cute! Where did it come from?"

"He's been abandoned," said Ella. "Someone left him in a cardboard box in the Country Park."

"Ella! What were you doing in the park? You're supposed to come straight home."

"I heard the puppy barking," said Ella. "He sounded upset. It's a good job we found him.

He's far too small to be out on his own. Can I keep him? Please, Mum?"

Ella had often asked if she could have a dog, but this time was different. She felt strangely drawn to the cuddly puppy sleepily snuffling in her arms. She couldn't explain it, but Ella knew they were meant to be together.

"He's very sweet." Mum hesitated. "Come indoors while I think about it."

"Please," Ella wheedled. "I've always wanted a dog and this one's special. Look how gorgeous he is."

"I don't know, Ella," said Mum. "It's a big decision. I'll have to talk to your dad about it first. He likes dogs, but he's not keen on having one, in case it messes up his garden."

At least Mum hadn't said no. Now all Ella needed to do was to persuade Dad to let the puppy stay. She was sure that once Dad got to see him he'd agree.

"Thanks, Mum." If her arms hadn't been full of puppy, Ella would have hugged her.

"Come on, Izzy. Let's make the puppy a bed and find him something to eat."

Isabel looked at her watch and pulled a sad face.

"I wish I could, but I promised Mum I'd help her with Billy and Jack. They're such a handful." Gently she stroked the puppy's head. "What'll you call him if your dad says you can keep him?"

"Blue."

Ella glanced at the puppy. The name had come out before she'd even thought about it, but immediately she knew it was right.

"Blue," said Isabel, trying it out. "Like his eyes."

"Blue looks like a type of husky dog," said Ella's mum thoughtfully. "Did you know they come from the Arctic?"

"A husky!" exclaimed Ella. "Wow!"

The snowflake on Blue's collar seemed to sparkle more brightly. Ella couldn't resist touching it, and there it was again. That feeling, like the snowflake was sparking with a strange sort of energy that made her fingers fizz. She closed her eyes and immediately saw a picture of six husky dogs pulling a sled across a snowy landscape. It was so real, Ella imagined herself riding with them, an Arctic wind whipping across her face, snow freezing on her eyelashes.

"Ella? I said, ring me when your dad gets in."

Isabel pulled on Ella's arm, tugging her out of her daydream. Shivers fizzled up and down her spine. That was amazing! Ella loved the magical white world with the sled pulled by snowdogs.

"I'll ring you," she agreed, going to the door with her friend.

As Ella went indoors, Blue began to stir. Yawning daintily, he opened his eyes and stared up at her. His look was so intense it felt as if he were begging Ella to let him stay. But

her dad was a keen gardener and every year his vegetables won prizes at the county show. Would Ella really be allowed to keep Blue?

"I'll find a way," she whispered. "I promise."